George H. Perkins

Report on the Marble, Slate, and Granite Industries of Vermont

George H. Perkins

Report on the Marble, Slate, and Granite Industries of Vermont

ISBN/EAN: 9783742819987

Manufactured in Europe, USA, Canada, Australia, Japa

Cover: Foto ©Andreas Hilbeck / pixelio.de

Manufactured and distributed by brebook publishing software
(www.brebook.com)

George H. Perkins

Report on the Marble, Slate, and Granite Industries of Vermont

...REPORT...

ON THE

Marble, Slate and Granite

Industries of Vermont,

● BY ●

GEORGE H. PERKINS, Ph. D.,

State Geologist.

RUTLAND:
THE TUTTLE COMPANY, OFFICIAL PRINTERS.
1898.

...REPORT...

ON THE

Marble, Slate and Granite

Industries of Vermont,

• BY •

GEORGE H. PERKINS, Ph. D.,

State Geologist.

———•————— —— —

RUTLAND:
THE TUTTLE COMPANY, OFFICIAL PRINTERS.
1898

OFFICE OF STATE GEOLOGIST,
BURLINGTON, VT., October 15, 1898. }

To His Excellency, Josiah Grout, Governor:

SIR:—In accordance with the requirement of Section 2, Act No. 7, 1896, I herewith present my Report on the quarrying industries of Vermont. By your kind permission I have been allowed to delay publication somewhat beyond the required time on account of my very recent appointment. It is needless to call attention to the haste with which the field work, preparatory to the Report, as well as the writing of the manuscript, have been done. Only about six weeks were available for both, and I have endeavored to make the most of this brief period.

Very respectfully,

GEORGE H. PERKINS.

REPORT.

EARLY last summer the State Geologist, Rev. G. W.
Perry, on account of continued and serious illness, re-
signed, and on the seventh of September I received, from
Governor Grout, my appointment to the office. I at once
proceeded to carry out, as far as possible, the requirements of the laws defining the duties of State Geologist,
especially those of Sec. 1, of Act No. 7, of the session of
1896, viz.: " The State Geologist shall, during the next
two years, personally inspect the mines and quarries now
in operation within the State; also deposits of minerals
of economic value, which have not been opened or developed;" as well as the following sections of the same act.
Obviously it was not at all possible to comply fully with
the requirements of the above act within the time remain-
ing before the session of the General Assembly, to which
a Report was to be submitted. Some limitation being thus
absolutely necessary, I concluded to confine my investigations and field work to the three greatest of our mineral industries, marble, slate and granite, and after several weeks
of very active field work, I found that it was not practicable
to visit all of those quarries from which these materials
were obtained. Most regretfully were quarries of soapstone and talc, mines of copper, beds of clay, ochre, lig-
nite, iron ore, manganese, and other interesting minerals
wholly ignored. All of these are well deserving of a full
Report, but this is out of the question at present.

It hoped that the present Legislature will make such
appropriations for the work of the State Geologist as will
make a continuance of the work begun in this Report

possible. This publication is not to be regarded as anything more than preliminary to a much fuller report, of
more complete investigation of the mineral resources of
our State, which investigations can be made, and a Report
which would be of great value, prepared at a very mod-
erate cost, during the next two years. It is neither to the
credit nor advantage of Vermont that no such report exists, and that full, accurate and scientific information
respecting the quarries, mines and rock formations, of
our State is nowhere to be found. The large Report on
the Geology of Vermont, in two quarto volumes, published in 1861, contains much valuable matter, and much
that is not very valuable, but it does not give such information as any one who is seeking to make profitable investments would require. And during the thirty-seven
years that have passed since that Report was issued, no
Geological Report has been authorized or published by
the State until the Act above referred to, passed by the
Legislature of 1898.

As has been stated, the illness of Mr. Perry, who had
collected considerable material for the purpose of
preparing a Report, prevented him from accomplishing
his purpose. Having no access to this material, the
writer could only attempt to carry out the intent of the act
as well as possible in the very few weeks at his disposal.
During the month of September I visited and examined
about seventy-five quarries, but none of them received the
careful attention which should have been given to them,
and it is with some reluctance that I present a Report
which necessarily falls far below what it might have been
had a few months more been available. On this account
it is important that this reconnoisance, for it has been
little more, may be followed by a thoroughly carried-
out campaign during the next two years. Such a geological study of our mineral resources, followed by a full
and well illustrated Report, would not only be interesting to those already interested in our quarries and
mines, but it should awaken interest in many quarters

now indifferent through lack of information, and, therefore, should do something to increase the resources and wealth of Vermont.

Vermonters should realize that there is no State in the Union which has, in proportion to area and population, so great wealth and resources in beds of useful rocks. If properly developed during the next ten years, the marble, slate and granite industries of Vermont will surpass those of other States. Vermont is known far and wide as an agricultural State, but we can scarcely hope to remain in the front rank in this respect. Our manufactures are varied and important, but we cannot rival many another State in these industries. When, however, it comes to the possession of vast beds of marble, slate and granite, and the production of stone from these deposits, our future outlook is most encouraging. The existence of such riches being assured, the first rational step toward developing and utilizing them is that which leads to a knowledge of what we have and to giving others, those outside the State, who have needed capital, some knowledge of what there is awaiting their investments. I do not think that there is a State in the Union which has greater need of a geological survey, or which would receive greater benefits from it than our own. Such a survey, if properly conducted, is really taking an inventory, an account of stock, of the natural resources of the region examined, and I believe that such surveys have almost always been of very great benefit to the State carrying them on, benefit far beyond all cost to the State. Vermont is behind most States in investments in scientific work, and she has suffered accordingly. Where such investment has not borne abundant fruit, the reason has been that scientific work has been entrusted to unscientific workmen, instead of being given to those properly prepared for it. There is very much work to be done in Vermont in the way of geological investigation. Besides the quarries and mines, there are most interesting beds of fossiliferous rocks

along the shores of Lake Champlain, and equally interesting masses of crystalline and metamorphic rocks in the
Green Mountains and from them on to the Connecticut
river, which presents many problems to the scientific in-
vestigator, and which should receive far more thorough
study than has hitherto been given to them. Aside from
the very valuable, but limited, studies of President Brainerd and Professor Seely, on the Marble Border of Vermont, and on the Calciferous and Chazy beds of the
Champlain Valley, of Mr. Walcott on the Cambrian beds,
of Mr. T. N. Dale on portions of Rutland and Bennington
counties, of Mr. S. P. Baldwin and Dr. C. H. Richardson on
the Pleistocene of the Champlain Valley, of Dr. Richardson
on Washington county, and the older but all-important
work of Rev. A. Wing on the Rutland marbles, little has
ever been done to really elucidate the many difficult problems which Vermont geology presents. It is no dispar-
agement of the above named writers on Vermont geology
to say their work is little more than the beginning of
what should be done*.

---

* The following list includes most of the papers on the Geology of
Vermont which have been published during the last fifteen years:

Geological Sections Across New Hampshire and Vermont. C. H.
Hitchcock, Bulletin American Museum of Natural History. Vol I, p.
155.

Notice of Geological Investigations Along the Eastern Shore of
Lake Champlain. Conducted by Ezra Brainerd and H. M. Seely. H.
P. Whitfield, Bulletin Am. Mus. Nat. Hist. Vol. I., p. 293.

The Marble Border of Western New England. By Ezra Brainerd
and H. M. Seely. Proceedings Middlebury Historical Society, Vol.
I., Part II.

The Winooski Marble of Vermont. G. H. Perkins. Am. Naturalist,
Vol. XIX., p. 128.

Studies on Cambrian Fauna. C. D. Walcott. Bulletin U. S. Geol.
Survey, 30.

The Original Chazy Rocks. E. Brainerd and H. M. Seely. Am.
Geologist, November, 1888.

An Account of the Discoveries in Vermont of the Rev. A. Wing.
J. D. Dana. Am. Journal Science and Arts. Third Series. Vol. XIII.,
pp. 332, 405. Vol. XIV., p. 36.

The very great importance of one branch of the geological work of which I have been writing, that which includes the deposits of useful and monumental stone and the quarries which are located upon them, is best understood, perhaps, when we consider that Vermont, though one of the smallest States in extent of surface, yet stands first in the value of marble produced, second in slate and second in granite, and third in the total of all quarry products, only Pennsylvania and Ohio producing more. The total value of all the stone produced in Vermont in 1897 is, according to data collected by Mr. Perry, $3,598,399. The capital invested was, in 1897, over $12,000,000, the exact amount I cannot ascertain, but I am sure that it is more than the above named sum. Over five thousand men are employed in the 107 quarries, and there are others not reported. It is very gratifying to learn from nearly all the quarries investigated that the demand for Vermont stone is increasing, and also that the supply is far from being exhausted. Many deposits have been scarcely touched.

Perhaps it may be well to state that while I shall find it convenient, even necessary, to mention certain quarries and quarrying firms, this is done in no way to advertise them, but only to make known, as best I can, the re-

The Calciferous Formation in the Champlain Valley. Ezra Brainerd and H. M. Seely. Bulletin Am. Mus. Nat. Hist. Vol III., p. 1.

Observations on the Fauna of the Rocks at Fort Cassin, Vt. R. P. Whitfield. Bulletin Am. Mus. Nat. Hist. Vol. III., p. 25.

The Chazy Formation in the Champlain Valley. Ezra Brainerd. Bulletin Geological Society of America. Vol. II., p. 293.

Structure of the Ridge Between the Taconic and Green Mountain Ranges in Vermont. T. N. Dale. Fourteenth Report U. S. G. S., p. 531.

The Pleistocene History of the Champlain Valley. S. P. Baldwin. Am. Geologist. Vol. XIII., p. 170.

The Chazy of Lake Champlain. Ezra Brainerd and H. M. Seely. Bulletin Am. Mus. Nat. Hist. Vol. VIII., p. 305.

Description of New Species of Silurian Fossils from near Fort Cassin, Vermont, and Elsewhere on Lake Champlain. R. P. Whitfield. Bulletin Am. Mus. Nat. Hist. Vol. IX., p. 177.

sources of the State and what is being done to develop them. I greatly regret that the brevity both of the time for visiting and studying the quarries, and also for writing this Report, makes it quite impossible to do justice to many important quarries. One of the many reasons why a more complete Report should be prepared in the near future, is that the deficiencies and unavoidable errors of this may be corrected. On this account the State Geologist will be very glad to receive any information respecting quarries or mines of this State.

Besides the great quarries of marble, slate and granite, Vermont has extended limestone quarries, a few of soapstone or steatite, one of talc of considerable value, beds of ochre, clays of various kinds, as well as mines. These lesser but important interests should by no means be neglected. A full Report should include them all, but for reasons already given they are not included here.

THE MARBLE INDUSTRY.

Vermont has long been famous for the quantity and quality of the Marble produced. The pre-eminence of Vermont in this respect is shown by the fact that in 1800 the marble obtained from the quarries in the United States was valued at $3,488,120, and of this Vermont produced $2,169,500, and I presume these relative values would not be greatly changed by more recent figures, which I am unable to obtain. In absolute quantity, New York exceeds Vermont, but much of its product is fitted only for use as a building stone, while much of our marble can be used in statuary and monuments, and therefore has a much greater value. No other State, nor the whole United States, can at all approach Vermont in the quantity and value of the finest grades of marble.

By far the largest part of the marble quarried in Vermont is obtained in Rutland County, though there are a few quarries just south, in Bennington County, and

Figure 1   Post Office and Court House, Montpelier.
Built of Sutherland Falls Marble

north, in Addison. There are deposits, not now worked,
in Chittenden, and quarries of the beautiful Champlain
marbles in Franklin County. There are, in all, between
thirty and forty quarries, in which are employed over two
thousand workmen, the Vermont Marble Company alone
employing 1700. The deposit of marble, so far as now
known, begins at the south at Dorset Mountain, and extends northward, in a narrow belt, through Wallingford,
West Rutland, Proctor, Pittsford and Brandon, to Middlebury, and there are unworked beds considerably north of
the latter place. These are true marbles, metamorphosed
limestones. The marble of Swanton and other localities
is of different origin, and geologically is not true marble,
though just as valuable as if it were, possibly more so. As
has already been noticed, the great advantage which Vermont has over other marble producing States is seen in
the quality of her marble. Marble good for building is
found in many localities, but it is worth only from 75 cents
to $2.00 a cubic foot, while marble suitable for monu-
ments sells at from $5 to $7, and statuary brings $12. As
the cost of quarrying a block of common building marble
is the same as if it were of finer grain, it is obvious that a
quarry, or deposit of the finer stone is greatly to be desired. Of this finer marble Vermont produces more than
seven times as much as does any other State. Nevertheless the use and increasing use of marble as a building
stone is not unimportant, for much of our marble is of
value chiefly for this purpose, either because of its texture or color. That marble, especially when "rockfaced," is capable of being used as a building stone, with
good effect, can be easily proved by reference to the U. S.
government building in Montpelier, a cut of which is,
through the courtesy of the *Montpelier Watchman*, here
given (Figure 1), as well as a view of the Water Tower at
Fort Ethan Allen (Figure 2), which, like the building
mentioned, is of Sutherland Falls marble. This latter
view was furnished by the Vt. Marble Company. Many
very fine buildings in various parts of the country are
constructed of the Rutland marbles.

Figure 2. WATER TOWER, FORT ETHAN ALLEN.
Rockfaced Sutherland Falls Marble.

Beginning our survey of the Marble region at Dorset, we find high up on the sides of Dorset Mountain a group, or belt of quarries, some of them not at present worked, which are capable of producing a large amount of fine marble. The largest and most productive quarry is known as Freedly's, carried on, as is the mill at the base of the mountain, by Messrs. J. K. Freedly & Sons. This is a very interesting quarry and one of the oldest, having been worked, it is said, since 1803. It is charmingly located on the east side of the mountain about 1000 feet above the beautiful valley. Dorset Mountain is capped by a mass of slate about 500 feet thick, and immediately below this is a great mass of marble, which is several hundred feet thick in some parts of the bed, though much less in other parts. Beneath the marble are great beds of limestone. The marble is rather more coarsely crystalline than that at West Rutland, and some of the layers are rather soft, but most of it is very hard and it is said to be durable. In the Freedly quarry the color varies from pure white, through several shades, clouded and veined, to dark bluish gray. The quarry is partly open and partly "tunnel," that is, the marble has been followed under the slate, leaving, as it has been removed, cavern-like spaces. This "tunnel" is quite large. I should estimate its breath at seven or eight hundred feet, depth from one hundred to a hundred and fifty feet, and height twenty-five. The massive roof is supported by massive columns left for that purpose. The open quarry is large and both produce abundance of good stone. From the quarry an inclined tramway leads down to the mill, a mile or so below. The track is double, so that a loaded car in descending, draws up an empty one on the other track. Most of the product of this quarry goes to Philadelphia. Going south along the east side of the mountain we soon reach a large quarry not now worked called the "Blue Ledge." A very pretty bluish marble is found here and the enormous dump heap shows the extent of past working. Still further south is a very promising looking quarry, also unworked, called the Folsom quarry. There appeared to be an abundance of good stone here awaiting the enterprise of some energetic quarryman. Going on to the southwest side of the mountain we find the Edison quarry which produces a finely veined stone in large blocks, but when sawed the sheets are very likely to be unsound. The quarrymen called my attention to a curious phenomenon which has also been observed in one or two quarries at Pittsford and Brandon. As the surface of the marble deposit is cleared, channelling machines are run back and forth across it until the bed, three, four, six feet deep, as it may happen, is cut into long strips, which are then cut across into blocks. In this quarry these strips when cut spring up from the bed below, so that it is difficult to work, as tools are caught and held. One of the northern quarries was abandoned, I was told, because of the trouble this springing caused.

Farther along the west side of the mountain is a large quarry which is just being opened by the Dorset Mountain Marble Company. There is here a splendid mass of marble of quite varied shading. Borings show a bed of marble several hundred feet thick and apparently very sound, but as to this only trial can determine, for even the most expert quarryman is unable to foretell whether blocks that seem perfectly sound as they are taken out, will prove so, when sawn. A few rods north of this new quarry is an older one formerly known as the Prince quarry, but now worked by the company just mentioned. Considerable marble has been taken from this place and it is still worked. One great obstacle which these Dorset Mountain quarries must overcome is their distance from railroads. Except the Freedly quarry, they must all send the rough stone by teams over a difficult mountain road for several miles. It is fortunate that the hauling is all down hill, so that large loads can be drawn. At the base of the mountain, in Dorset, there are several quarries now abandoned. The largest of these, and one which was once very actively worked, is that of Kent & Root. This, with the large mill, not far off, now stands deserted and desolate.

So far as I know, marble was quarried at Dorset before it was obtained in any other locality. Says Professor Seely in "The Marble Border of Western New England," to which I am indebted for numerous valuable suggestions and facts: "The first quarry opened at Dorset was by Isaac Underhill in the year 1785 on land owned by Reuben Bloomer and still held by the Bloomer family. The quarry was first wrought for fire jambs, chimney backs, hearths and lintels for the capacious fireplaces of the day. People came a hundred miles for these beautiful fireplace stones and considerable trade in them soon sprang up. Other quarries were soon in operation and from 1785 to 1841 nine quarries were opened."

North of Dorset there were formerly quarries in North Dorset, Danby and Wallingford, but none of these are now worked. Most famous of Vermont marble beds are those at West Rutland, and the name Rutland marble is used in trade to designate either that from these quarries or from Proctor. In this region there are in all about thirty quarries, most of them worked.

Twenty-five of these are controlled by the Vermont Marble Company, which is said to be the largest in the world. The West Rutland quarries are in two groups. Most of them are on the west side of a north and south ridge, extending about half a mile and the stone from these is mostly quite light in color, while a mile and a half north on the same ridge are two quarries which produce no light marble, but a very fine dark stone. There is here a vast deposit of unusually sound and desirable stone, and on the opposite side of the valley there are other fine deposits not worked. The marble is in beds, or layers, which dip to the east at varying inclinations from 20° to 80°, the average dip being given as about 45°. The beds are together from 50 to over 100 feet thick. The quarries here are really great pits. There is a rectangular opening perhaps 200x250 feet, and the walls descend vertically, or nearly so, to a depth of 200 or in some cases 300 feet.

The first or "covered quarry" is 300 feet deep, and there are two tunnels about 200 feet long, running under the cliffs. Blocks of almost any size which can be moved by the hoisting machines can be obtained from these quarries. The marble in some quarries varies but little from layer to layer, while in others there are several varieties in a single layer. Some layers produce pure white statuary, others most daintily veined or clouded, show a white ground variously streaked, blotched or veined with green, in one bed, blue in another, yellow or light brown in another, olive in another, and it is easily seen that the mixtures and relative amount of these veins in the white ground may be innumerable. I do not know how many shades are recognized in trade, but in the State collection there are blocks which represent twenty varieties. It is said that in one of the West Rutland quarries there are "fifteen different layers varying in thickness from two feet to ten, and varying also in color, texture and value."

The following section, taken from the Eighteenth Annual Report of the U. S. Geological Survey, will aid the reader in understanding the structure of these quarries :

Blue marble, top ⎫ White marble ⎬	30	feet
Green striped	2	"
White statuary	5-8	"
Striped monumental	2-8	"
White statuary	8 0	"
Layer partly green, partly white	4	"
Green and white "Brocadillo"	2½-8	"
Crinkly, silicious layer, half light, half dark	2-8	"
Light and mottled	4-6	"
Green striped	6 in.	
White	2½	"
Half dark green, half white	8-0	"
Italian blue	18-20	"
Mottled limestone	—	

FIGURE 5. MARBLE MILLS AT WEST RUTLAND

Figures 3 and 4 give a good view of some of the marble mills in which the stone is sawed and cut, and

FIGURE 4. MARBLE MILL, WEST RUTLAND.

figure 5 is a rather poor illustration of some of the quarries, which I introduce here because, though not as good as could be wished, it gives a better idea than words alone of the character of these quarries. I am indebted to the Tuttle Company for these illustrations.

Figure 5. INTERIOR OF QUARRY AT WEST RUTLAND.

The two northern quarries, the Esperanza, worked by the Vermont Marble Company, and the True Blue, worked by an independent company, are in the same bed of dark, richly veined and clouded marble, which is very effective for interior work. It seems to be a compact, hard, and durable stone.

VIEW FROM THE SUMMIT AND DOWN BLACK. Photo.

Going around, or over this ridge, we find on its eastern slope the old Sutherland Falls quarry at Proctor. Figure 6, though not showing the quarry, is taken very near it,

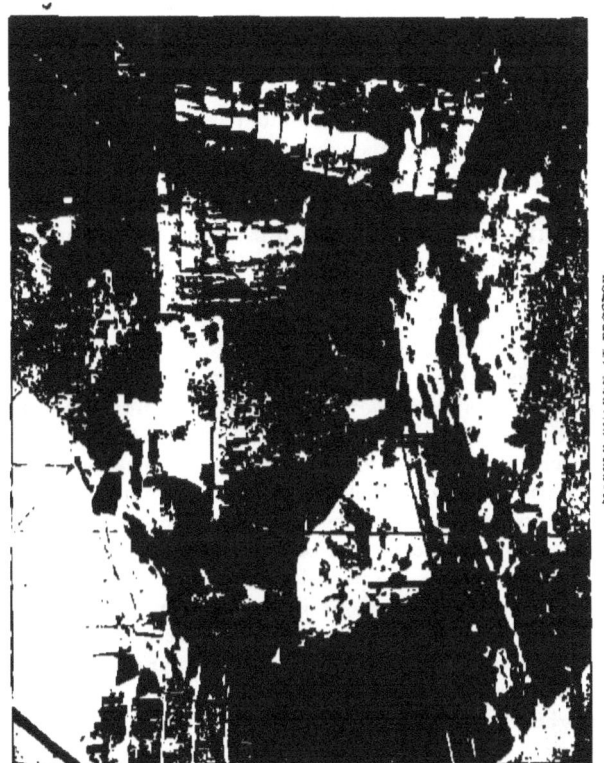

MARBLE QUARRY AT PROCTOR.

Figure 7. SUTHERLAND FALLS QUARRY, PROCTOR.

and shows blocks taken from it. Through the courtesy of
Mr. Spear, I am able to give the accompanying illustration of this famous quarry, said to be the largest quarry in
the world. Its impressive proportions do not appear in
the illustration, which, like all those of quarries, fails to
represent the magnitude of the object. This quarry is
located in what appears to be a gigantic pocket, or mass of
marble enclosed in limestone on all sides. An immense
quantity of marble has been taken from it, and at present

the walls at the highest point must be 200 feet high, and the area of the floor is three acres. The beds of marble are nearly horizontal, though there is an evident anticlinal arrangement. The marble is mostly rather light, though the dark " mourning vein " is quite dark. These " mourning veins" found in this quarry are very fine. The markings are numerous, almost black, and very wavy. Of this Prof. Seely writes in the " Marble Border": "It would be interesting to know the origin of these mourning marbles, in which the white and black are so curiously mingled, The material giving the black appearance is undoubtedly carbon, and probably in character approaching the graphite, which marks the coarsely crystalline limestone of the Adirondack region. When freely exposed to a high heat the dark color disappears, leaving a white line. A conjecture might be ventured that the rock was originally of different chemical composition in the different parts; in the white the oxidation of the carbon was complete during metamorphism, while in the dark the oxidation was interfered with. A second conjecture would be that during the metamorphism, the particles of carbon moved together and became aggregated, as in the Adirondack marble. The first suggestion is supported by the actual difference in the character of the dark and white portions, the former carrying with it insoluble silicious minerals. A further thought suggests itself, whether the darkly mottted marbles will not be found to be metamorphosed Black River limestone of the New York geologists." I have already noticed that the thickness and extent of the layers in some of the quarries is such that very large blocks can be obtained. Figure 8 shows one of the buildings of Princeton University, built of Sutherland Falls marble. The columns in front of this building are turned from a single block, and they are twenty feet long and three feet in diameter at the base. One of the large groups of statuary on the Boston Post-office is carved from a single block of the same marble. In the falls of Otter Creek at Proctor the Vermont Marble Co. have a convenient and most valuable

Figure 8 — CLIO HALL, PRINCETON UNIVERSITY — Built of Sutherland Falls Marble.

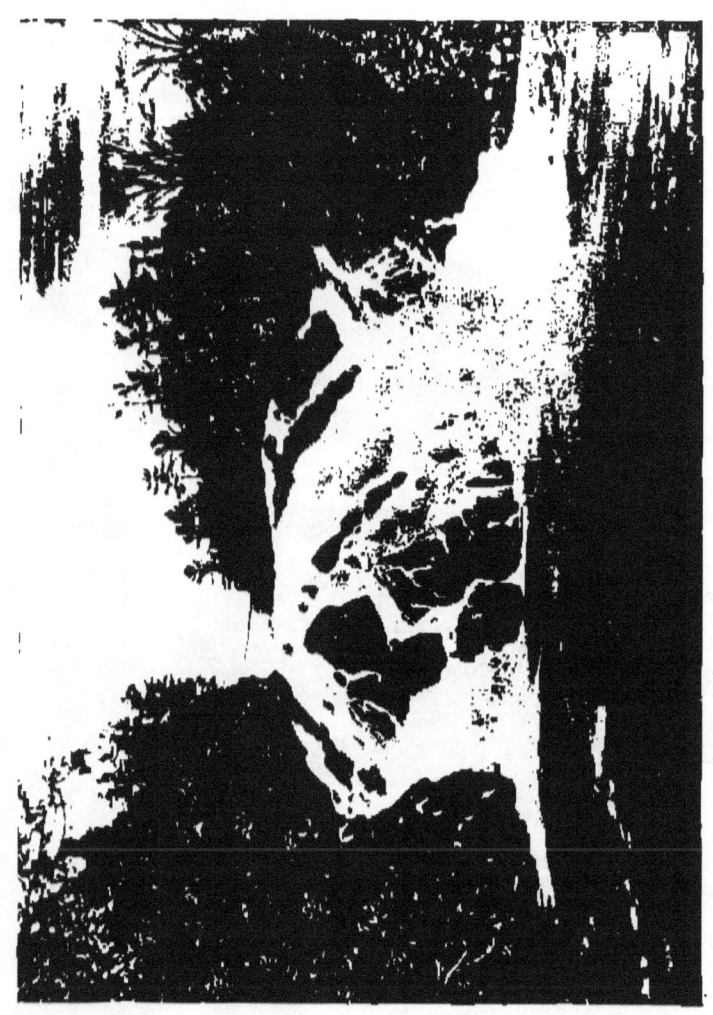

FIGURE 9. FALLS OF DEEP CREEK. PHOTON.

source of power by which to run their mills, for it is
obviously cheaper to use water power than steam. These
falls, which are well shown in the illustration (Figure 9),
supply from 2,000 to 2,500 horse power.

North of Proctor, and between that place and Pittsford, are several quarries, not now worked, and one of
considerable importance called the "Mountain Dark,"
which is in operation. As the name indicates, the marble
is of dark bluish color. It is, however, troublesome on
account of frequent flaws. Very much of the marble
quarried is troublesome and unprofitable on this account,
and even in the best quarries the waste is considerable.
As has been seen, the quality of the marble cannot always
be accurately determined by an inspection of the blocks,
and therefore it not infrequently happens that an appar
ently sound block is transported to the mill and sawed
into slabs before its real character is ascertained. If then
it be poor, there is not only the loss of the stone, but of
all the labor which has been expended upon it. Within
the limits of the marble region it is not difficult to find
abundant marble. The main trouble is to find that which
is sound and perfect when worked. Small specimens are
of little value as indicating the soundness of larger pieces,
and no one should be misled by them. Almost any quarry
will furnish a square foot or so of sound marble, though it
may never yield any larger pieces. Several miles north of
the Mountain Dark quarry, there are several quarries in
Pittsford, all producing a dark marble. It is a handsome
stone, but quite liable to imperfection, though good blocks
are by no means unattainable.

Quarrying was carried on in Pittsford quite early,
not so early as at Dorset. The oldest quarry was opened
in 1795. According to Professor Seely, in the "Marble
Border," there are three beds of marble in Pittsford, extending north and south. "The most easterly of these
has a breadth of about 200 feet, and on it was opened, in
1871, the quarry known as the Central Vermont quarry.

It was successful until the great depression of 1874, from which it has not yet rallied. The marble is of the same character as that at Proctor, of which bed it is probably a continuation. The middle bed is separated from this easterly one by about 200 feet of lime rock. This bed is itself 400 feet wide and contains marble of different shades, from pure white to a dark blue. Buildings made of this marble have stood the test of years. * * * The third or west bed, thought to correspond to that of West Rutland, is about half a mile west of the Central and abuts on the west against the slate, this having disappeared from all the region east of it. This bed, about 400 feet wide, holds beautiful dark blue marble, mottled and veined." In this last named bed there are two considerable quarries, the Hendee, worked by the Vt. Marble Company, and the Florentine, the stone from which is sawed at Beldens Falls.

North of Pittsford I found no quarries in operation until reaching Brandon, where there are at present two, besides several not worked. I was told that the Corona quarry, still farther north, was also worked.

About two and a half miles southwest of Brandon station is the Bardillo quarry and mill. Here there is a peculiarly elegant stone, quite unlike any other that I have seen. The very numerous, strongly-marked, narrow veins which traverse the blocks in sinuous or zigzag lines, in quite unique fashion, and yet with a certain regularity, make this a very handsome stone. It varies in shade from light to dark gray. The quarry is not large, but the supply seemed to be good and the beds were thick and solid. The quarry was opened, the workmen tell me, in 1882. Most of the product is worked up on the spot into monuments. A much older quarry is that known as Brandon Italian, which is nearer town, being about half a mile below the station. The Bardillo quarry is located on a hillside, and the stone is quarried, thus far without going to any great depth. This other quarry is much deeper, and

is peculiarly long and narrow. The beds are thick; at
the time of my visit the channeling machine was cutting
out a bed 6 ft. 8 in. in thickness. The mill which had
been operated at the quarry burned last winter and the
company are building a new one at Middlebury, to which
place the blocks will hereafter be taken to be worked up.
This marble is solid, and light colored, that is, white with
dark veins.

There were formerly several quarries in Middlebury,
but none are now worked. I have spoken of the loss
which always attends marble quarrying, because of the unsoundness of much that is obtained. Throughout the marble belt good marble is never found near the surface.
Hence, when a quarry is opened in a ledge, a greater or
less, but always considerable, mass of waste stone, earth,
etc., must be removed. For this reason every one who
undertakes to open a quarry must spend a considerable
sum before he can begin to look for returns. This is well
stated in a pamphlet published by the Vermont Marble
Company: "A marble deposit being found, it is first
bored, and with a machine constructed for the purpose,
a solid core is taken out, from which the quality of the
marble is easily determined. The soundness, however,
can only be proved by opening; and the opening of a
marble quarry, unlike granite, is a laborious and expensive operation. From forty to seventy-five thousand dol-
lars has been spent upon several of the West Rutland
openings before stock that would even pay to saw has been
taken out. The quarry being stripped of the top rock,
channeling machines, driven by power, are put on and the
entire quarry floor cut into strips, a cut being also made
at each end. Small holes at intervals of a few inches are
then bored into the bottom of the layer, by means of machines constructed for that purpose, and called gadding
machines, and into these holes are driven iron wedges.
In this way all of the layer that has been cut is freed from
its bed, and it is not unusual to see a strip of rock 50 ft. or
more in length raised in this manner. The layer is then

in the same way broken into blocks of the size desired, and the marble is hoisted from the quarry to the bank by huge derricks, and if of suitable quality, sent to the mill to be sawed."

Many interesting questions arise as to the origin, age, etc., of the marbles of the region we have been considering. Only very briefly can these be discussed here. As to the origin of these marbles, not of all those kinds of stones sold under the name, but of the marbles in the Rutland district, geologists are agreed that they are metamorphosed limestone. That is, that the ordinary dark, fossiliferous strata, such as we now find at Larrabees Point or on Isle la Motte, has been, in the marble region, softened, heated, compressed, crystalized until transformed into the non-fossiliferous, light colored marble. As to the age of these marbles, we may speak with confidence, because of the investigations of a Vermont geologist, who is almost unknown in his own State, the Rev. A. Wing of Whiting, who died about 20 years ago. Mr. Wing, by dint of most careful study of the marbles and ledges of Rutland County, established their age beyond doubt as of the Chazy limestone, one of the lower members of the Ordovician or Lower Silurian. That is, the marble is of the same age as the limestones of the southern portion of Isle la Motte, at Fisk's and Fleury's quarries. Although most of the beds, as those at West Rutland, are of this age, it may be that some are older, and some, as Prof. Seely has suggested, are newer. Chemically, limestone and marble do not very widely differ. Lime carbonate is the chief component of each, but there are some important differences. In the 18th Annual Report of the United States Geological Survey, several analyses of Rutland marble are given. A single example must suffice for the present:

	BLUE MARBLE.	WHITE MARBLE.
Silicate of Alumina	.39	.62
Carbon dioxide	44.00	43.80
Lime	55.15	54.95
Magnesia	.57	.59

The above shows that there is little difference between the dark and light varieties, in the substances which compose them. In the same Report we find the following:

"Vermont is likely to remain in the first place for the production of fine marble for many years to come, in spite of claims of superior product which are occasionally made in connection with new discoveries elsewhere;" and also the statement that the "marble of West Rutland and its vicinity is as yet without a peer in the United States for the finest uses to which marble is applied, and it supplies a large proportion (elsewhere stated as 81 per cent) of the stock used for cemetery work."

Aside from the great quarries and mills with their hundreds of workmen and vast output which have been mentioned, there are in Vermont other quarries which produce marbles of which we may well be proud. The marble quarried on Dorset Mountain has much of it been taken to Manchester to be worked, hence outside of the State it is often called Manchester marble. There is no quarry of true marble in Manchester, but there is a quarry of breccia, which was sold as marble, but which is no longer worked because of its unsoundness. It is a very interesting and handsome stone, quite unlike any other in the State. It is composed of fragments, of different sizes, of red, gray, white or brown stone, cemented together by a dark red material. Were it only sound it would be a very attractive stone for interior work.

What are known as the *Champlain Marbles* are quite unlike any found elsewhere in the United States. They differ materially from the true marbles in that they are not metamorphic, but are substantially as originally deposited. They belong to an older period geologically than the white marbles and are much harder.

All are highly colored and all take a most brilliant polish. The prevailing colors are white and various shades of red, from dark red-brown to delicate flesh color. Olives

and light greens are also sometimes seen in certain layers.
They belong to a geological formation known as the red
sandrock, which is, in age, middle cambrian. This formation extends from Canada through northern Vermont south
as far as Shoreham. It is not of great extent from east to
west, but forms a narrow band near the shore of Lake
Champlain and approximately parallel with it. Many of
the head-lands on the eastern side of the lake are of this rock.
Most commonly it is a hard, dark red sandstone containing
besides large percentage of silica, eight or nine per cent of
potash, about the same of iron, and more or less of lime.
The composition of the rock is not uniform, but differs
greatly in different portions even of the same stratum.

The color, though chiefly dark red, is sometimes light
red or even reddish-buff. Moreover the entire formation,
which is about two thousand feet thick, includes limestones,
dolomites, slates and shales, though the red sandrock is, in
most places, by far the most conspicuous member of the
formation, and forms the greater part of its thickness.
Still, in some localities other beds make up a not incon-
siderable portion of the whole, as the following section
taken at Swanton by Sir William Logan, and given here
with some modification, shows :

Feet.

1. White and red dolomites (Winooski marble) with sandy layers;
—some of the strata are mottled, rose red and white, and a few
are brick red or Indian red. Some of the red beds contain
Ptychoparia adamsi and *P. vulcanus*............. 870

2. Gray argillaceous limestone, partly magnesian, holding a great
abundance of *Palæophycus incipiens*...................... 110

3. Buff sandy dolomite.. 40

4. Dark gray and bluish-black slate, partially magnesian, with thin
bands of sandy dolomite. The slate contains fossils as *Kutor-
gina cingulata*, *Orthisina festinata*, *Camerella antiquata*,
Ptychoparia teucer, *Olenellus thompsoni*, *Mesonacis vermon-
tana*... 180

5. Bands of Bluish mottled dolomite, mixed with patches of gray
pure limestone and gray dolomite and bands of gray mica-
ceous flagstone with fucoids 60

A mile or so north of the above section, other strata occur as follows:

6. Light gray more or less dolomitic sandstones and "some of which are fine grained, others are fine conglomerate." These are interstratified with bands of white sandstone........................ 630
7. Bluish thin bedded argillaceous flagstones and slates, containing *Conocephalites arenosus* and fucoids................... 60
8. Bluish and yellowish mottled dolomite 120
9. Yellowish and yellowish-gray sandy dolomite.................. 600

Still further north, on the Canada line, there are additional strata, though not well exposed, but in general Sir William gives them as follows:

10. Buff and whitish sandy dolomite, holding a great amount of black and gray chert in irregular fragments of various sizes up to a foot in length and six inches wide. There are also masses of white quartz. Thickness (conjectured)..................... 790

Most of the layers are not fossiliferous, and in few are fossils abundant. It may be true that fossils are really more common than they seem to be, for they only occur as casts, and, with the exception of the Algæ, these are rarely visible except when the surface of the stone has weathered so as to leave them in relief, and of course this happens only occasionally. Near Burlington, where the stone is extensively quarried for building purposes, some of the layers exhibit abundant casts of Algæ, together with mud cracks, ripple marks and other evidences of shallow water formation. Farther north, at Georgia, and still more to the north, at Highgate, various trilobites and Mollusca have been found of the genera Oleuellus, Ptychoparia, Camerella, Orthisina, Obolella, etc. (see No. 4 above). The dolomitic portion of the beds constitute what has long been known as the "Champlain" marble.

The beds of "marble" appear first one or two miles north of Burlington and extend in a somewhat interrupted series north, through St. Albans and end at Swanton. Some of the layers are quite distinct from the red sandrock proper, others pass into it by imperceptible gradations. Ordinarily the marble beds are far less siliceous than the main bulk of the sandstone, often containing only one-seventh as much silica as that usually contains, or even less, but they are always much harder than ordinary marble. Analyses of the marble have been made, but cannot be of great value when applied to the whole mass, because the relative proportion of the substances composing it is extremely variable.

Identical results would scarcely be obtained from analyses of any two specimens taken at places a little distant from each other. Silica is always present, usually about ten per cent, lime carbonate forms from thirty to forty per cent, and magnesia carbonate about the same, while iron and alumina form a smaller portion of the mass.

No fossils had been discovered in this portion of the formation until a few years ago, when looking over a pile of sawn fragments—refuse from the mill at Swanton—I noticed two or three pieces which contained evident fossils. These were afterwards identified by Mr. Billings of the Canadian Geological Survey, as *Salterella pulchella*, described by him from the Straits of Belle Isle, and not hitherto known from Vermont. It is only with difficulty that this fossil can be detected in uncut pieces of marble, but when blocks which contain specimens of it are sawn they are quite noticeable, as they are pure white and imbeded in the red stone, appear as small thimble-shaped, oval, conical or circular bodies, as they are cut in one or another direction. It seems probable that the *Salterella* occurs throughout the dolomitic beds, for I have found it at their extreme limits near Burlington and Swanton. The fossil is, however, not common anywhere. It occurs in patches sometimes as large as one's hand, scattered over the slabs here and there. Other fossils also occur in marble, but are not so well defined as to be certainly identified.

More than thirty years ago the beauty of the mottled dolomite attracted the attention of marble workers, and a quarry was opened about six miles from Burlington, and

(8)

some of the blocks of stone taken out were sent to New
York and Philadelphia to be sawn into slabs and polished.
The results were, I believe, satisfactory in every way except financially. The stone made beautiful slabs for table
tops and mantels, but its hardness, while adding to the
beauty of the polish which it received, rendered the sawing and finishing so costly that after a short time the attempt to place it in the market was abandoned.

Quarries were also opened, many years ago, near
Swanton, and these are still operated by the Barney Marble Company. The Swanton quarries are about a mile and
a half southeast of the village, on the east bank of the
Missisquoi river. The deposit here is extensive and
forms a considerable ridge extending along the river,
from the west side of which the stone is quarried very
conveniently. The layers dip some 20 to 30 degrees
to the southeast. The quarries are mainly surface quarries, and thus far the excavation has nowhere been very
deep. The beds are of good thickness and very fine.
Sawed blocks can be readily obtained. I measured some
of these blocks that were lying near the derrick at the
time of my visit. One was 9 ft. x 4 ft. x 4 ft; another 12
ft. long and less regular in form. Most of the blocks were
of the common size found at all the quarries, viz.: 6 ft.
or 8 ft. long and 4 ft. x 4 ft. at the ends. Blocks 16 feet
long have been quarried and worked up. Indeed, the capacity of the derricks and the possibility of handling large
blocks is all that determines the size of those quarried.
All of the stone must be hauled by teams to the mill at
Swanton, where the fine water power afforded by the
falls in the Missisquoi, is well utilized by the company.

This marble has been used in many public buildings
in different portions of the country, notably in some of the
corridors at the capitol at Albany, as wainscoting, and also
in the new wing of the Astor library in New York. It
should be noticed here that while this marble is unrivaled
for inside work it is not well adapted to situations in which

it is exposed to the weather, as its colors fade and its beauty is greatly impaired when thus exposed. There seems to be great inequality in this respect in blocks from different layers. At least this is indicated in the appearance of blocks that have been for some years lying about the quarries. Some of these appear to be but very little changed, while others have their surfaces reduced to a nearly uniform yellowish-red. No one need fear any change in the appearance of polished slabs when protected from the inclemency of the weather.

Perhaps the most remarkable characteristic of the Champlain marbles is the wonderful variety of shade and general appearance which they present.

Not only may slabs which are quite unlike each other be obtained from a block as it is sawn parallel with the stratification or transverse to it, any variation in the direction of the saws giving variety in the slabs; but even the opposite surfaces of the same slab may differ greatly. The rock in some of the layers is a more or less complete breccia, white or light-colored fragments being enclosed in a dark red paste. These fragments are of all sizes, from those several inches long and wide to those no larger than the head of a pin. In some cases several adjacent bits were, when first held in the paste, one large piece, and subsequently broken, as the fractured edges of each exactly correspond to those of the pieces next it. The brecciated structure is conspicuously perfect in some blocks and quite imperfect in others, and it finally passes into what was evidently a pasty mass of nearly uniform fineness before consolidation took place. Some of the beds appear to have been much more thoroughly worked over, and the materials more completely ground and mixed than others, and the different varieties are in part due to this.

While but few colors are seen in the different layers, nevertheless these are mingled in such varying proportions as to produce unlimited diversity. Shades of red

are especially abundant, so that almost every conceivable
tint is found; less common are green, chiefly in olive
shades, drab and rarely yellow, all mingled more or less
abundantly with white.   The different specimens may
conveniently, though without absolute exactness, be ar-
ranged in several series.   One of these would embrace
those slabs in which the red, which in most cases is the
predominating color, is clear and decided.   In this series
we have many varieties, from those in which the red is
like that of jasper, or what is known as Indian red, to
those in which it is simply a delicate pink, like the lining
of a shell.   Another series gives us the red always of a
brownish or chocolate cast, and this is sometimes very
dark.   This in turn passes through all intermediate shades
to almost white.   In a third series the red shades are less
conspicuous, and with them are mingled greens and
greenish-drabs or sometimes lavender shades.   It is easy
to understand how endless variation may be produced by
varying combinations of these different shades with white.
This is true both in the blotched and in the shaded layers.
Those which show the brecciated structure more or less
clearly vary as the fragments are large or small, and
whether many large are mingled with many small or the
reverse, and whether many large light fragments are
mixed with dark small ones, or large dark bits with small
light ones, and in the clouded or shaded layers light bands
and blotches may predominate in one slab and dark bands
in another.   It will be obvious that no description of such
marbles can convey to those who have not seen them very
clear ideas of their appearance.   More than thirty varieties of this marble have been named by one company or
another, but most of these are not used.   There are six,
more commonly placed upon the market by the Barney
Company, though, of course, others can be supplied if
desired.

The Mallett's Bay beds of this marble, alluded to on
a previous page, have been repeatedly worked, and some
fifteen years ago a company called the Wakefield Marble

Company invested considerable capital in quarrying, erection of mills, and placing the marble on the market. They were obliged to use steam power, which was one reason of the failure of the undertaking. The hardness of the stone and consequent slow progress which saws and other tools make in working it, render the relative cost of steam and water power very unequal. Although this enterpise, so thoroughly begun, has not been successful, I cannot believe that the great beds of beautifully colored marble which exist at Mallett's Bay are never to yield profit.

Messrs. Fisk & Bradley have this year opened a new quarry in the same formation as that in which the Barney quarries are located. A great variety of colors is found here and the outlook is very promising.

There are large beds of a light drab limestone in and about Swanton and extending south to St. Albans, which is extensively quarried and burned to make lime by Messrs. J. P. Rich at Swanton and W. B. Fonda at Swanton Junction, large quantities of lime being produced by these gentlemen. But in addition to this use of the stone, large blocks are quarried, which are taken to the mill and sawed, to be finished as "Swanton Dove" marble. The delicate drab of the general mass of the stone is varied by veins of pure white, thus producing one of the neatest marbles in the market.

Perhaps the most elegant marble which is quarried and finished in Vermont is also produced by the Barney Company. It is a very fine verde antique, most superbly veined in various shades of green, with veins and blotches of black and also of pure white. It is very hard, being a serpentine, and receives a very high polish. For many sorts of interior work nothing can be more effective than this verde antique, but it is difficult to work, and for that reason is more expensive than any other kind. The quarry from which this stone is obtained is at Roxbury. It was

worked many years ago and some large pieces taken out,
and then for years it lay deserted, until a short time ago
the Barney Company took it in hand, and have since done
considerable work in getting out the stone. As now
opened, the quarry is not a large one. It is located on the
east side of a considerable hill, about half a mile south of
the station, near the railroad. So far as developed, the
the bed of marble, or serpentine, is 12 to 16 feet thick,
but the bottom has not yet been reached. Immediately
above the marble is about 20 feet of greenish schist. At
the north end is a bed of white talc. Green talc, actinolite
and asbestus are also found in the quarry. Some large
blocks have been gotten out. I saw at the mill blocks 9
feet long and three feet square at the ends. Some of
these are very dark, others quite light.

In the town of Washington a dark bluish siliceous
limestone is quarried which, when finished, is very handsome. It is peculiar in shading, and in those blocks which
are abundantly intersected by darker veins is of very strik-
ing appearance. Dr. F. A. Warner has not only opened
a quarry, but built a mill in the village, where the stone is
cut and polished. At the time of my visit, there were
some beautiful specimens of the marble in various monuments, slabs, etc., at this mill. I am greatly indebted to
Dr. C. F. Richardson, instructor of geology at Dartmouth
College, for the following notes concerning this marble
and the region in which it occurs. Dr. Richardson has
repeatedly and carefully studied the part of the state
referred to in his notes, and they are especially interesting
because very little trustworthy information respecting the
geology of eastern Vermont is to be had: "The Washington limestone is, in general, a dark gray, siliceous rock.
The coloring matter is uncombined carbon. In the southern and western portions the limestone is darker and contains many beds of plumbaginous mica schist. The deposits at Wait's River closely resembles the Columbian

marble of West Rutland, which is of the same age. The alternation of light and dark bands of highly crumpled strata, together with the beautiful polish which the rock receives, makes it eminently suitable for ornamental work.

At Washington more than twenty quarries have been opened since the discovery of the marble five years ago. It lies horizontally in sheets from ten to one hundred feet in length. Throughout the entire town the formation exceeds 5,000 feet in depth. The rock hammers white, and the polished letters stand out in such bold relief that it is legible at a greater distance than the inscription upon any granite." The contrast between hammered and polished surfaces is greater than in any stone I have ever seen. Chemical analysis of the stone gives most remarkable results. It seems like a general mixture of all the reagents in a laboratory.

Dr. Richardson sends in the following analysis of two specimens of this marble:

	Sample A.	Sample B.
Silica, SiO_2,	35.748	35.748
Titanic Oxide, TiO_2,	.100	.180
Carbon Dioxide, CO_2,	22.860	23.870
Ferric Oxide, Fe_2O_3,	.010	.010
Alumina, Al_2O_3,	0.113	0.112
Ferrous Oxide, FeO,	.940	.941
Glucinum Oxide, GlO,	.813	.815
Manganic Oxide, MnO,	.070	.075
Baric Oxide, BaO,	.210	.210
Calcic Oxide, CaO,	27.803	27.804
Magnesic Oxide, MgO,	8.248	8.244
Sodic Oxide, Na_2O,	.186	.187
Potassic Oxide, K_2O,	.068	.064
Lithic Oxide, L_2O,	.823	.824
Water, H_2O,	.108	.107
Phosphorous Pentoxide, P_2O_5,	1.859	1.859
Chlorine, Cl,	.307	.807
Fluorine, Fl,	.026	.020
Carbon, microscopic trace	....	....
	99.883	99.892
Less O, Cl. & F	.079	.079
	99.806	99.813

The Washington limestone, like the marble at West Rutland, was undoubtedly once regularly stratified, fossiliferous rock, but it has been to a certain extent metamorphosed and the fossils obliterated. Dr. Hitchcock has found fossils in rock of the same formation at Derby and Dr. Richardson in the marble at Wait's River. Dr. Richardson writes: "The most abundant palæontalogical evidence is in the Canadian territory at Willard's Mills, Castle Brook, Magog, Quebec, where many species of graphtolites occur in great abundance. The slates in which they occur are lithologically homogeneous with the roofing slates of Montpelier and Northfield. These slates, the Bradford schist with its patches of limestone and the Washington limestone with its peculiar beds of biotite and plumbaginous mica schist, are lower Silurian, and, more specifically, lower Trenton." These observations are very interesting and important, because the rocks involved cover a larger area than any formation in the State. They are found over much of that portion which lies between the Green Mountains and the Connecticut River.

On Isle la Motte there are extensive beds of limestone, some of the layers of which have been used as marble. Some of this is black, some gray, the latter mottled on account of the presence of numerous small fossils or fragments of large ones. One of the oldest quarries in the State is the Fisk quarry, on the southwest side of the island. It is said to have been opened before the Revolution. It is near the shore of the lake where there is a dock, to which a tramway runs from the quarry. The accompanying illustration, furnished by courtesy of *The Vermonter* (Figure 10), gives a fair idea of this quarry.

Figure 50 Fisk's Rock and Quarry, Chazy Limestone, Isle La Motte.

An immense quantity of stone has been removed
from this quarry, for, although the walls are not high,
I should think nowhere over 20 feet, yet the upper
layers have been removed over an area of six or seven
acres, if not more.   The strata of Chazy limestone are
nearly horizontal, the dip being only a few degrees to
the northwest.   The stone is black, or very dark, compact and solid, and has been, as it still is, in demand
for bridge piers and foundations.   The large black blocks
from some of the layers when sawed make a good black
marble. which is known in trade as Fisk black.   There
are also gray beds which produce a marble called " French
Gray."   This stone was largely used in the piers of the

great Victoria bridge. Some of the beds are two feet
thick, others six, eight or ten. In this quarry fossils
are not abundant. Most conspicuous are masses of
stromatocerium. Maclurea magna is also not infrequent,
and orthocerata and other fossils now and then occur.
The stone is evidently a deep, still-water deposit, which
has been to some extent uplifted, but not otherwise
much disturbed. A short distance southeast of Fisk's
quarry is another large one known as Fleury's. This
is a lighter colored stone, most of it being gray. The
strata are not as thick and are more fossiliferous than
those at Fisk's, and are somewhat older. They belong
to the older layers of the Chazy limestone, and are
near the Calciferous. The layers contain numerous
brachiopods as orthis, strophomena, camerella, trilobites as asaphus, cheirurus, and illænus and some corals.
There is also a dock and tramway here for loading the
stone. The strata are somewhat more disturbed than at
Fisk's, but the dip is not very great. The whole southern
end of Isle la Motte is made up of lower and middle Chazy,
in many places wholly uncovered or only partly covered by
a thin layer of glacial drift. Over these nearly level or
only slightly dipping strata, one may drive for a mile or
two north to Goodsell's quarry, on the eastern shore of the
island. The beds here have been worked deeper, so that
the bottom of the quarry is considerably below the general
surface, while at Fisk's or Fleury's one may drive directly
from the road into the quarries and over the floor, especially at Fisk's. The rock at Goodsell's quarry is gray,
with maclurea and stomatocerium, and apparently is
middle Chazy. A thorough study of the geology of Isle
la Motte would be to a geologist a most interesting task,
for it is a region which affords many attractive localities,
which invite investigation. In a paper published by the
American Museum of Natural History, Bulletin, Vol. VIII.,
p. 305, President Brainerd and Professor Seely have given
a brief account of their investigations on the Island. They
found that the total thickness of the Chazy was 834 feet.

At the southern end there is a little Calciferous rock, and in the center are Trenton beds.

THE SLATE INDUSTRY.

More than fifty years ago a writer spoke of Vermont as "justly celebrated for its roofing slate," but at that time there were apparently few quarries and a not large production, and yet even then, 1845, some quarries had been worked forty years. In those early days an important part of the business of a slate mill was the manufacture of the now obsolete school slate, and, from softer layers of slate pencils.

The great slate region of Vermont is in Rutland County, but slate has been obtained in Northfield and Montpelier, and in Benson in considerable quantity, but is now quarried only to a small extent.

In the slate belt of Rutland County there are over sixty concerns engaged in the slate business. All of these do not own or work quarries, but some operate several, so that it is within bounds to state that between fifty and sixty quarries are, or recently have been, worked in this one county. It is not easy always to ascertain the precise number of quarries in any given vein, for the term is not always used with the same meaning. The best definition of a slate quarry was given me in the office of Messrs. Norton Bros. at Granville. It seems that the common lease of a slate quarry includes a strip of land twenty rods wide. Therefore, originally a slate quarry must be a part of the ledge of this width, and perhaps of the same or less length, the width being reckoned along the slate ridge. By some of the men, each pit was called a quarry and this might do very well were it not for the fact that in course of years of quarrying several adjacent pits are no longer separated, but, the wall of stone between having been removed, they are continuous. Others consider each derrick a quarry and count the quarries by derricks.

However we may choose to reckon the quarries, no one can visit the region from Hydeville through Poultney to Pawlet without being convinced that they are very numerous.

This slate belt begins with the Lake Bomoseen quarry at Cedar Mountain, six miles north of Fair Haven, and extends southward through Poultney and South Poultney to Pawlet, a distance of about twenty-five miles. Contiguous to the Vermont region is that of Washington County, New York, and the whole is geologically one. Most of the offices of the quarries at Pawlet are in Granville, N. Y., and several of the companies operate quarries in both Vermont and New York.

A few of the quarries are located on the side of a hill and are more or less surface quarries, but most are rec-

Figure 11. Slate Quarries.

tangular pits. The quarry is begun on top of a ridge and the slate followed down at a high angle, or even perpendicular, for one, two, or three hundred feet, the average depth being no far from 150 feet. On account of this

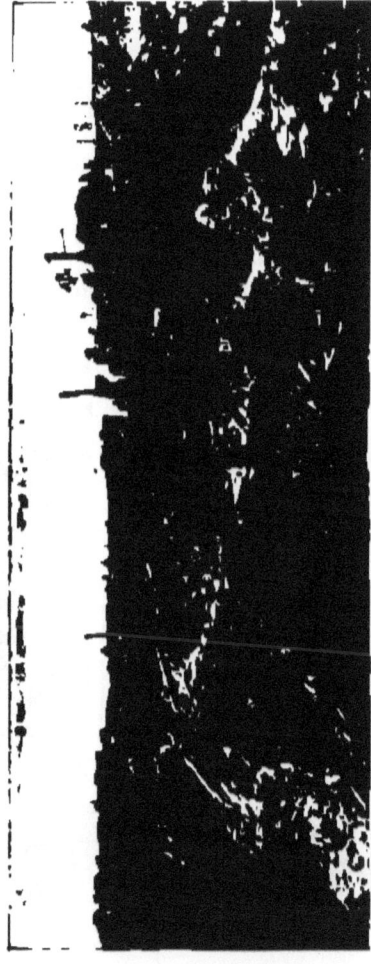

Figure 12. SLATE QUARRIES

character, good views of slate quarries are not easily
obtained and I am unable to show any that are satisfactory.

The accompanying illustrations, figure 11, loaned
by Hon. V. I. Spear, Secretary of the State Board of Agriculture, is about as good as any. This, with the other
illustration, figure 12, which shows one of the larger quarries at South Poultney, which The Tuttle Company
furnished, will help one to some idea of the appearance
of the slate region, about the quarries.

The most northern quarry is the Lake Bomoseen,
six miles north of Fair Haven. It is very near the
shore of the lake and large pieces of slate can be
loaded on boats and thus be transported to the railroad or mills at Hydeville. This quarry, which produces a fine purple slate, is a surface quarry, the slate
being taken from the side hill. The quarry is at some
distance from any that are now worked, but formerly
there were extensive quarries and millsat West Castleton, a mile or so southwest, but they became unprofitable, and what was a scene of busy activity is
abandoned and desolate. Still farther west and south
there are several quarries now worked with good promise
of increasing business. Between these quarries and
Hydeville is a locality known as Scotch Hill. Here there
are two quarries of fine purple slate. At the Humphrey
quarries, or rather at the mills, I saw the finest large
slabs that I found anywhere. This firm produces only
large pieces, or what is called "mill stock." The adjacent
quarry, owned and worked by Mr. J. Williams is peculiar
in that its product is not worked up at all, but is sent in
the rough to mills at Hydeville. The beds here are very
thick and of excellent quality. After leaving Scotch Hill
we find no more quarries until we are beyond Hydeville.
Here are several large quarries, beginning with that of
the Blue Slate Company. Here some roofing slate, but
much more "mill stock" is produced. Beyond this
quarry is a series of large ones extending through

"Hyde's Patch" towards Poultney. One of these, the Eureka, is said to be the largest in the State. North of Scotch Hill, there was a quarry known as the Old Harvey, in which were beds of what is known as "Unfading Green" slate, and at the Eureka we find the same in greater quantity. This seems to be really a green slate which keeps its color, for in the piles of waste I could see no difference between fragments that had lain a long time exposed to sun and storm and those which had only lately been thrown out. This Unfading Green is in great demand in England, and I was told at several quarries where it is found, that half of what they produce is exported. The Eureka quarry produces from 1500 to 1800 squares of roofing slate a month. Besides the green, purple and variegated slate is obtained at this quarry. Quite similar to the Eureka are two large quarries, one on each side of the road to Poultney. These are the Lloyds, and beyond this, quarry follows quarry until we reach Poultney, or near it, and then there are no more until we reach South Poultney, where there is a group of nine or ten large and long worked quarries. In these, while the slate is mostly of the variety known as "sea green," a light green, but not unfading, there is also much purple and variegated, and in one quarry, Griffith & Nathanaels, there is a bed of very dark gray, called in trade "Poultney gray," which resembles the Maine black slate. At the Auld & Conger quarry at this place, several of the original pits have been worked into one, very long, narrow and deep. A few miles south of these is the largest group of all, I should think, called, from a switch and side track from the Delaware & Hudson Railroad to the quarries, the "Switch quarries." Here the quarries follow each other along the ridge for about two miles. All are very near the New York line, and I believe that most of the offices of the various companies are in Granville, N. Y. All of these quarries produce only roofing slate, mostly of the sea green variety, there being very little purple found in any and none at all in most. There are, I judged, about

twenty quarries in operation in this group.   The last
quarry in the group is, as are all the Switch quarries,
in the town of Pawlet.   This is the Rising & Nelson.
It is on top of a considerable elevation, and is the deepest
quarry which I saw.   The workmen said that its depth
was 300 feet.   The slate here is all sea green, and the
vast dump heaps indicate long working, and it is probably
one of the oldest of the quarries.   I was obliged to make
a much more hasty examination of all these quarries than
was at all desirable.   I visited over thirty which were
being worked, but many important ones were passed by.
The Hughes and Norton Brothers quarries are large and
interesting and substantially like those just described.
During the last few years the market for most kinds of
slate has been dull and prices low, partly, if not wholly,
because the great quarries of Pennsylvania, added to those
of Vermont and New York, overstocked the market and
thus checked the demand.   No other state except Pennsylvania produces nearly so much slate as Vermont, but
that state far exceeds us.   Of late, however, the business
is reviving and the demand increasing.   All of the slate
producers of whom I inquired agreed that their business
was decidedly improving.   This is also shown by the
opening of new quarries and the investing of new capital.

It is interesting to note the difference in the color of
the slate in different quarries, or rather in different parts
of the slate belt.   This has been noticed incidentally
already, but a review of the whole region will make the
fact more evident.   At the quarry on Lake Bomoseen, at
Cedar Mountain, there is little else than the purple, which
occurs there in fine beds, though there is some green.
South from here, just beyond West Castleton, both purple
and unfading green are found.   Still further south, at
Scotch Hill, only purple, and although unfading green
and variegated, that is, purple more or less blotched with
red, occur in considerable beds at Hydeville and Hyde's
Patch, purple is very abundant, and so on to South Poult-

ney, when the sea green becomes more abundant, and
little purple occurs in most of the quarries, and there is
the bed of "Poultney gray" mentioned above, which
occurs only in one quarry. Beyond South Poultney, in the
great group of "Switch quarries," the slate is almost wholly
sea green. It may be noticed that the unfading green and
the sea green, though very similar in color and appearance,
differ in texture and chemical composition, one, as the
name rightly indicates, enduring exposure without change,
the other fading if much exposed. The fine red slate
which is in constant demand for roofing and which therefore brings a much higher price than other colors, is found
only in Washington County, N. Y. It is exceedingly tan-
talizing to an ardent Vermonter to ride through the slate
belt and be constantly forced to notice how invariable the
red beds are on the New York side of the line. For a
dozen miles or so beds of red slate occur on the New York
side, in full view of one standing in Vermont, and time
and again reaching almost into our State, but never coming
quite across the border. It would seem highly probable,
since this is all one slate region, that at any time beds of
red slate may be found on our side of the line, but thus
far all search for them has been in vain. In all the quarries it is necessary to remove not only the glacial drifts
which covers the whole country, but the upper layers of
slate are of no value, and it is sometimes necessary to take
off 20 to 50 feet of these top layers. The blocks of rough
slate are removed from the beds, so far as possible, by
wedges and bars. Blasting is, of course, at times necessary, but is resorted to only as a necessity. The blocks
when detached are hoisted and placed on cars, or wher-
ever they are to be further reduced, by very ingenious and
specially adapted apparatus, worked by steam power. The
blocks are often large and maybe very irregular. The beds
in different quarries seemed to me to vary considerably in
the manner in which they could be broken. Some broke
into quite regular masses, others only in very irregular
fashion. If roofing slate is to be manufactured the large

(4)

blocks are broken into smaller, until those approximating
the size of the slate wanted are obtained. Various sizes
are used, but in most of the quarries I found that slates
10x20 inches were most in demand, especially abroad.   A
skilled workman takes one of the blocks and very deftly,
using a wide chisel and mallet, splits it first into several
thick slabs and then each of these into the thin slabs,
which, when trimmed in a machine with a large revolving
knife, become roofing slate.   When, instead of this, " mill
stock " is wanted, the process is, naturally, quite different.
In this case larger blocks are quarried and with correspond-
ing care.   These are hoisted and placed upon the bed of a
sawing machine, where they are cut into regular form.   If
necessary, the surfaces are planed or otherwise smoothed.
The manufacture of slabs for billiard tables, stair treads,
platforms, and the like, seems to be limited to comparatively few quarries, and chiefly those in northern part of
the slate belt.   Some, as that at Cedar Mountain and those
on Scotch Hill, produce no roofing slate; others, as the
Blue Slate Company, produce both roofing slate and mill
stock, while the series of large quarries at South Poultney
and Pawlet produce almost wholly the roofing slate.

At present the annual production of slate in Vermont
amounts to about $850,000 and from 1,400 to 1,500 men
are employed.   Most of the workmen in the slate quarries
are Welsh, and some of the owners are also Welshmen.

Slate has been obtained at Benson, but I was not able
to visit that locality, and can make no report concerning
it.

The only slate quarry which is now worked in the
eastern part of the state is at Northfield.   In years gone by
a considerable amount of good slate has been obtained from
this place, and I see no reason why profitable quarries may
not be operated here, though before expressing any decided opinion I should wish to examine the ledge much
more carefully than I have thus far been able to do.   Formerly there were four or five quarries, but only one is now

in working order. This is about two miles southeast of
the village, and is being vigorously worked by the Dole-
Brill Slate Co. Unlike the quarries of Rutland County,
this produces sound stone almost to the surface, so that the
waste is very little. The slate, like all that of Northfield,
is of excellent quality—strong, unfading, and of a fine
dark color like the black Maine slate. The color is not
like that of any of the slates of Rutland county except the Poultney gray of Griffith & Nathanaels, to which
it is similar, though darker. There seems to be an unlimited supply of this slate in the ledges about Northfield.
As we have seen, this slate is lower Silurian in age, as are
those of Rutland county most probably.

THE GRANITE INDUSTRY.

It is but few years since Vermont had any reputation
as a granite-producing state, although the existence of extensive granite ledges has been well known ever since the
state was settled. In the first Report on the Geology of
Vermont, which was published in 1845, granite is only incidentally mentioned and not a single quarry is particu-
larly noticed, though there were then a few of no great importance. Probably the largest quarries were then, as
now, at Barre, for the State House was built in 1837 from
Barre granite, and this was probably very much the largest
contract taken by a granite quarry in Vermont until perhaps ten years ago, when, after slowly increasing for many
years, the granite business, chiefly at Barre but not wholly,
suddenly increased to unexpected proportions.

In 1880 Vermont produced, according to the Census
Report, 187,140 cubic feet of granite, which was valued at
$59,075. In 1889 the production was 1,073,580 cubic feet,
valued at $895,510, and in 1897, according to statistics col-
lected by my predecessor, Mr. G. W. Perry, the granite
produced by 87 companies was valued at $1,512,543. In
1880 Vermont ranked thirteenth among granite-producing

states; in 1890 our state had advanced to the ninth place, in 1896 to the third, only Massachusetts and Maine producing more, and in that year the latter state did not produce nearly as much as Vermont did last year, and Massachusetts but about 0 per cent. more. As I have no reason to think that the output of granite has increased in these two states as it has done in our own, I think it safe to assume that at present Vermont is at least second in the amount of this stone sent out, and that if she is not already first, she very soon will be, for there are no signs that our granite industry is abating its progress and development, but, on the contrary, new quarries are being opened and old ones more actively worked than ever. If the above is true, Vermont now leads the country in marble and granite, and is second only to Pennsylvania in slate.

Granite beds are more widely scattered over the state than those of either marble or slate. Marble especially is limited to a few comparatively restricted areas. Nearly all of the slate, too, is obtained from the quarries of Fairhaven, Poultney and Pawlet, though the Northfield deposits are considerable, and there are smaller patches in other places. The great beds of granite are at Barre and Woodbury, and these I think are parts of the same vast deposit and no such deposit is to be found elsewhere in the state, if anywhere in the country. Hence these beds will always be the most important. Smaller deposits, however, exist, and most of them have been worked at one time or another.

These are found at Beebe Plain, Derby, West Concord, Greensboro, Chelsea, Groton, Ryegate, Williamstown, Northfield, Bethel, Sodom, Victory, Kirby, Morgan, Norton Mills, Dummerston, and perhaps elsewhere, and a syenite at Windsor. I do not mean that granite is now quarried in all these towns, for that is not the case, but it exists in all, and has been at one time or other quarried in all. So far as I can ascertain, there are about seventy firms

in the state concerned with either quarrying or manufac-
turing granite, many do both.

All of our quarries are open, and most, or many, surface quarries. An exposed ledge is attacked and the stone
removed. Unlike marble and slate, the granite is not unsound near the surface, though better at a considerable
depth below it. Hence there is little or no waste surface
material to be removed at greater or less expense. This,
as well as the nature of the quarries, makes quarrying
much cheaper in the granite region than it is in either the
marble or slate belts. I regret that the time which I could
take for inspecting the granite quarries was so short that I
cannot hope to do them justice. Many I could not even
look at, much less examine with the care they deserve.
Again I must refer to a future report for a more adequate
treatment of this most important interest. For the present,
as in the rest of the Report, I can only do so much as has
been practicable under the peculiar circumstances of my
appointment. I visited such quarries, I have introduced
illustrations as could most readily be found.

Granite is a composite of three common minerals—
quartz, which is much the same as flint, feldspar and mica,
or isinglass. The quartz is usually transparent or glass-
like or it may be white, the feldspar is usually a dull white,
the mica is generally black. The color, or rather shade,
of granite is due chiefly to the relative amount of mica
present. The very light or nearly white granite, like
Barre white, of which only a small amount is obtained, is
light because the mica is much of it light colored. Light
granite of trade is a light gray, the mica not being specially prominent in the mixture, though abundant. More
dark mica makes a medium, and much a dark or very dark,
if the black scales are unusually abundant. This is true
of Vermont granites which are all gray. I do not know of
any red granite in the state.

As to its origin, granite is probably much of it of vol-
canic or igneous formation. That is, it is molten matter

which has surged up from below the surface in great volume and cooled, crystallizing during the process. Geologists are more and more numerously inclining to the opinion that a large part of the granites are formed in this way. Other granite, which can not be distinguished from that of igneous origin, is formed from sedimentary rocks by metamorphism in a manner somewhat similar to that already noticed in the discussion of the origin of the Rutland marbles. I think that we have good reason to believe that our Vermont granites, or at any rate those of Barre and Woodbury, were formed of this last mentioned process, and that these granites are transformed lower Silurian, with perhaps some Cambrian strata. That is, the limestones and sandstones of these periods have been heated, softened, squeezed and crystallized into the granites, just as these same strata have, by a variation in the process, become the schists and gneiss of the Green Mountains and eastern Vermont.

It seems probable that both granite and marble will be used in increasing quantities as building stones. Granite, as has been mentioned, is quarried more economically and the rough stone is therefore cheaper than marble. Its greater hardness, however, makes it more difficult to work, and therefore more expensive in the finished, sawed and polished monument or column than is the softer marble. This latter stone is said to be coming into use more and more extensively for monuments in the South, where the milder climate does not affect it, but in the more severe Northern climate granite stands the test better, and is becoming increasingly popular for the construction of large and costly monuments and mausoleums.

Moreover, the bright, clear color and enduring quality of the Vermont granite are bringing it into favor as never before. In several very rigid and thorough comparative tests which have been made recently, Vermont granite has proved superior to any other tested. Perhaps the increase of the granite industry in Vermont is best shown by the facts in regard to the growth of Barre, for there is no reason to suppose that this, for a Vermont town, phenomenal progress, is due to anything else than the development of the granite quarries and the money which this has brought to the town. In 1880 the population of Barre was 2,000, and the property valuation was about $700,000. In 1890 the population had increased to 6,790 and the property valuation was $3,500,000. The population is now estimated at not less than 10,000, and the value of property is considerably larger than in 1890, and the past year has been one of unusual prosperity.

For facts regarding the granite works at Barre I am indebted to quite a number of residents of that place, but especially to the *Barre Enterprise* and to Mr. W. C. Olds. The latter has been at considerable trouble to look up statistics. He considers the present value of the annual output in these quarries to be not less than $1,000,000, taken as it leaves the quarry, unworked. Just how many quarries there are at Graniteville and the neighborhood, four miles east of Barre, I cannot ascertain, but there must be between fifty and sixty. About 100 derricks are in use, and 2,000 men, mostly Scotchmen, with a few Italians, are employed in the quarries and finishing shops, or "stone sheds," as they are locally called.

I have already spoken of the fitness of Barre granite for use either as a building stone or for the most costly monument. That this fact is appreciated all over the country is well shown by the following facts. This granite was used in the construction of the Grant monument in Lincoln Park, Chicago. Many of the finest soldiers' monuments have been made of Barre granite: Of the same material are made the Leland Stanford mausoleum at Palo Alto, which cost $100,000; the Goodrich monument in Rose Hill Cemetery, Chicago, costing $85,000; the great crucifix, said to be the largest ever made, at the entrance to Pine Hill Cemetery, Buffalo. These, and the list might be indefinitely extended, are constant witnesses to the beauty and excellence of the Vermont granite.

Figure 18. Surface Quarry, F. L. Taynton & Co., Barre.

Granite has long been quarried in this region. According to an article in the illustrated edition of the *Enterprise*, one Robert Parker, a revolutionary soldier, first opened a quarry, but not until 1875, when Barre was connected by a branch line with the Central Vermont Railroad, was any extensive work done. So far as I am aware, the first building of importance to be constructed of Barre granite was the State House, built in 1837. The stone for this was delivered in Montpelier for twenty cents a cubic foot, while to-day the same sells at the quarry for from seventy-five cents to $1.00 a foot. From a few tons annually, the amount produced has grown, as we have seen, to large proportions. A single firm shipped in 1896 10,000 tons, and 1,000 tons have been sent over the road from the quarries to Barre in a single day and 100,000 tons in a year. It is stated that if all the buildings and yards used in and about Barre for cutting and polishing granite were combined they would cover fifty acres. The actual terri-

tory in which the quarries are located is not large. Mr.
Olds writes: "The quarries are all within a radius of less
than a mile, and certainly not more than five per cent. of
the area within this radius is quarry land." The accompanying views of granite quarries will aid the reader in
understanding the conditions of the region and its quarries.

Figure 14, which was loaned by Hon. V. I. Spear,
secretary of the Board of Agriculture, shows very well
two of the quarries, a large block on the truck, a method
of transportation still in use to a considerable extent, for,
notwithstanding the existence of a railroad from Barre to
the quarries, built by some of the granite companies at a
cost of $240,000, a great many tons are drawn by teams.
In the upper right hand corner of this figure is a very good
illustration of some of the "stone sheds" in which the
rough granite is cut, carved or polished. Figure 15 shows
one of the larger surface quarries. For this I am indebted
to the Montpelier *Watchman*.

Many quarries are like this, others are deeper, though
none go down very far. One of these large quarries is
said to be sixty-five rods long and sixteen rods in average
width, and covers eight acres. Figures 16 and 17 show
two of the quarries of E. L. Smith & Co., by whom the
blocks were loaned.

Figure 16 shows unusually well what is also shown
in the quarry of Milne & Wylie in figure 14, namely,
the very thick bed of stone found in some of the quarries.
Figure 17 shows one of the quarries of C. E. Tayntor &
Co., by whom the block was loaned. There seems to
be no limit to the size of blocks which may be quarried
from these beds, except the capacity of the derricks, and
some of these are of great size. Figure 18 shows a steel
derrick in one of the Tayntor quarries, which is said
to be one of the largest ever made. It is ninety-nine
feet high, with a boom that has a sweep of seventy-
seven feet. It is rated at sixty tons, but the owners
claim that it will raise more than this. A mile of wire

Figure 15. A Large Granite Quarry. Wholly a Surface Quarry.

Figure 16. THICKBEDDED QUARRY. E. L. SMITH & Co., BARRE.

rope is used in connection with this great derrick. There
are others of nearly equal size in other quarries. With
the aid of these and other appliances for moving great
masses of stone and special cars for their transportation
to distant cities some very large blocks have been sent out.
One of the pieces in the Leland Stanford mausoleum
weighed, when finished, fifty tons. The block from which
the crucifix mentioned above was carved weighed, in the
rough, 160 tons. Another monument, though not all in
one block, weighed 210 tons. The largest single piece
which had ever been quarried at Barre before this season
is shown in Figure 19.

This was from the Tayntor quarry, and was, in the
rough, 51 feet x 4 feet x feet, and weighed 150,000 pounds.
It was worked into a shaft which is now in Greenwood.
Another block nearly as large was quarried by Barclay
Brothers, and is shown in Figure 20. This was 46 feet x

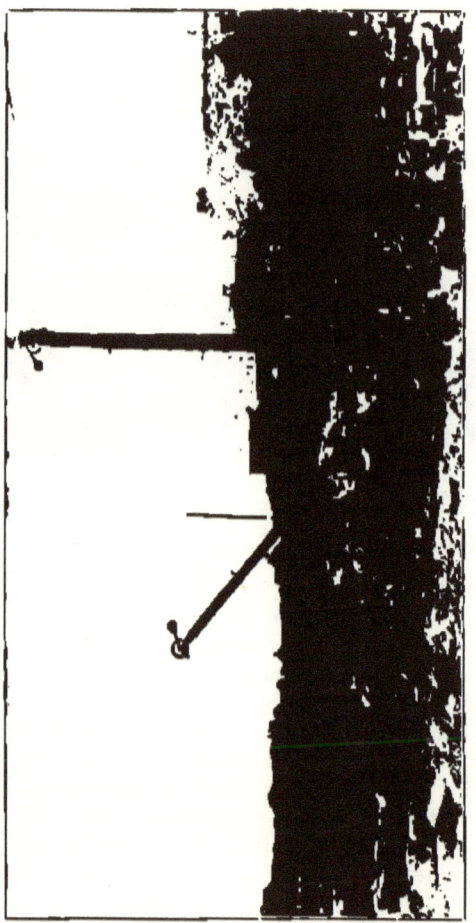

FIGURE 21. DARK GRANITE QUARRY. F. L. SMITH, BARRE.

1 feet x 1 feet.   Figure 21 showed a single block which weighed forty-six tons.

A shaft larger than any mentioned was quarried this summer by Wetmore & Morse Co.

Figure 18. Steel Derrick, Taystor & Co., Barre.

About twenty miles north of the Barre granite beds
are those of Woodbury.   The beds here form a small
mountain, and are, therefore, enormous in quantity. Most
of the works where the stone is cut and polished are at
Hardwick, six miles west, or between Hardwick and
Woodbury.   On this account the stone is often called

Figure 19. BLACK WISCONSIN 150,00 LBS. QUARRIED BY TAYLOR & Co. BANK

Hardwick granite. I was able to visit only two of the six quarries in operation, and these I examined less carefully than I wished to do. I am indebted to Mr. E. R. Fletcher for facts concerning this granite region. The quarries here were opened only ten years ago, and therefore the industry is not yet greatly developed. There are at present 220 men employed in the six quarries and probably a much larger number in the

FIGURE 20. SHALE FORTY-SIX FEET LONG QUARRIED BY BARCLAY BROTHERS, BARRE

Figure 21. Forty-six Ton Block, Barre Granite.

" stone sheds."   About $300,000 worth of granite will be
produced the present year. The stone lies in great sheets
in the Fletcher quarry, and the layers are nearly horizontal and are very easily removed, and the blocks are raised
by derricks, which swing them around on to cars standing
on a track which runs by the quarry, for a railroad has
been built from below Hardwick, where it reaches the
track of the Portland & Ogdensburg to and among some
of the quarries.

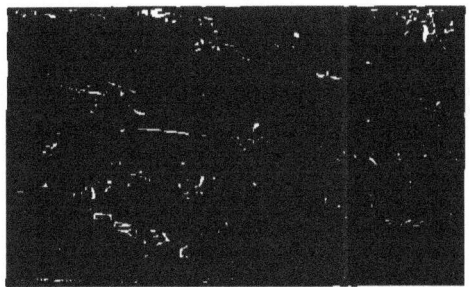

Figure 22.   QUARRY OF THE WOODBURY GRANITE COMPANY, WOODBURY.

At the foot of the mountain and below the Fletcher
quarry, which is near the top, is the quarry of the Woodbury Granite Company, a small illustration of which is
given in Figure 22.   I could not make any comparative
tests, but I could not see much difference between this
granite and that at Barre, and, as I have already in-
timated, I regard these beds as of the same general mass.
The Hardwick granite has been subjected to very severe
Government tests this season, and has proved superior
to others tested at the same time, and, as a result, the
granite for the monument to General Sherman is to
come from Woodbury.

At Ryegate the Blue Mountain Granite Company are
working a small quarry and are about to open a new one
in Tapham, just beyond the Groton line. Other quarries
and works are reported as not running.

There is an important quarry in the southern part of the state at Dummerston, carried on by the G. E. Lyon Granite Company of Brattleboro. The stone produced by this quarry is of two kinds, a light and a dark, both of good quality. Figure 23 gives a rather meagre idea of this quarry.

Figure 23. QUARRY OF G. E. LYON CO., WEST DUMMERSTON.

There were taken out there during the past season 147 blocks of granite, each 7 ft. x 5, 7 ft. x 3 ft., to be used in constructing the great dam at Holyoke, Mass. The granite from this quarry is especially good for paving streets, as it does not wear smooth. Mr. F. G. Rogers writes of this quarry: "Our quarry is a sheet quarry, operated at present by an overhead cable, capable of handling twenty tons per load and conveying ordinary sizes of stone at the rate of 600 tons per day. It is 1,500 feet long and is elevated by two towers, one 104 feet high and another fifty feet high. An average of 130 men have been employed during the past season, and we have orders to ast nearly, if not quite, through another season."

What is called "Ascutney granite" has been quarried at Windsor. This is really not a granite, but a syenite, which is much that is called granite in trade. The mica of granite is replaced by hornblende. The stone is very hard, darker colored than any of our granites, and I doubt not durable.

I have already expressed my belief that Vermont has much prosperity before her if she will only make the most of her best resources, as seen in marble, slate and granite quarries. A correspondent who is in the best possible position to know, writes: "The granite industry in Vermont is only in its infancy, and the time is not far distant when Vermont will lead the world in the production of fine granite. The importance of the industry and the value of these deposits within the state have been ignored most by the people of Vermont. Foreigners and foreign capital have done the developing mostly." The sinews of quarrying are the same as the sinews of war. Money, capital, this is what the quarry interests of Vermont most need. After a quarry is well under way money begins to return, as the history of Barre well proves, but no successful quarry can be put in operation without large, and, at first, unremunerative outlay. The one most uniform expression of need that I heard at many quarries was that of more capital, and it was a call often well warranted by the condition of the quarries. There are quarries which would swallow up all capital invested as completely as if it were cast into the sea, but there are others which, if they could be further developed, would yield a much greater profit than at present.

Undoubtedly, here, as elsewhere, money will be lost and hopes disappointed because of the failure of what seemed promising quarries. Caution is well everywhere, but I think it is especially necessary, if one is to escape disaster, when investing in quarries or mines. Nevertheless, I believe that much wealth is to come to Vermont through the further development of her quarries, and that many profitable investments will be made. A well planned survey is only preliminary to investment, it is true, but it is a most important preliminary, and one that may prevent much financial loss, if it does not, as it may, secure financial gain.